Simple
is
Ample

Neeraj Deginal

Clever Fox
PUBLISHING

Chennai • Bangalore

COPYRIGHT

From the author of the book

Zero Debt

Break the Debt Cycle and Reclaim Your Life

Contents

Gratitude

I am lucky to be alive and healthy. I am blessed to have family, relatives, and friends. I am thankful I have food, water, and shelter. I am blessed to have a great boss, colleagues, and organization. I am fortunate, privileged, and lucky. Thank you all.

With Gratitude

Simplicity is the ultimate sophistication.

– Leonardo da Vinci

Preface

I've always preferred to live a straightforward and simple life. But occasionally, I, too, became irrational. My consciousness was brought back to simplicity — thanks to the teachings of life.

Complicated things make me a little uncomfortable. It is just who I am. I prefer an easy-going, simple, and comfortable life. I feel contented and happy as a result. I have a lot of tolerance, yet sometimes fret over little things. So, maintaining my comfort level and avoiding stress truly becomes crucial for me.

With this book, *Simple is Ample*, I hope to drive home the idea that a simple life is all that one needs. Life does not need to be complicated.

Simple: easy, uncomplicated, basic, plain

Ample: enough, plentiful, sufficient, adequate, abundant

I am celebrating 11 years of debt-free living this year. A significant personal incident (more on this in my previous book *Zero Debts: Break the Debt Cycle and Re-Claim Your Life*) helped me realize that I needed to put an effort in this area, and I began my focused path to simplify life in 2008. Sorting out personal finances was the starting point and a key step in simplifying life. If you haven't read that book yet, I urge you to do so because it might serve as a prequel to this one and help you relate to it more easily. However, you can read this book on its own too.

In this book, I share the steps I took to simplify my life. The goal has always been to make life easier and simpler, especially in this increasingly complex world.

In my previous book, I had a whole chapter dedicated to life simplification. Taking it a notch further, I am devoting this book to explaining how 'simple is ample'.

By reexamining situations and taking the required steps (including *Minimalist* and *Essentialist* approaches) to simplify, I've been attempting to make life *Simple, Uncomplicated, Effortless, and Fulfilling*.

Most of the steps I've taken are the result of transfer of knowledge and vicarious learning. To understand how others handle situations and try to learn from them. I have been reading a lot of books, articles, and watching videos in this regard. I attempt to absorb knowledge from others' experiences and apply it to my own. Some are functional, but others require adjustments. Many of those lessons are listed in this book.

Although each chapter stands alone, they are all connected by the general concept of life simplification. Any chapter can be read in any order.

Anyone can read this book. I am sure there is something for everyone, and hope it helps.

Chapter 1
Personal Finance

*E*veryone, or at least most of us, work for money. Thus, personal finance plays a crucial role in our daily and long-term lives. Personal finance includes earning, saving, investing, and spending.

My first step in simplifying my life was to streamline my finances. Since 2011, I have been debt-free, and have taken several important steps to establish a solid financial foundation. Here are some financial areas I worked on to simplify my life:

Managing Debt

I cherish every second of it being debt-free. It feels relieving and empowering at the same time.

My first book, *Zero Debt*, was inspired by my own debt struggles and how I overcame them to lead a simpler, less stressful life.

I am sure you have heard several accounts of people struggling under the weight of debt, particularly in instances where we have little control over the outcome, such as losing a job, losing a business, experiencing a tumultuous pandemic, incurring unforeseen medical costs, etc. These situations don't just affect individuals; we've also seen businesses struggle with debt and fail because of excessive debt.

During the pandemic, we witnessed how our entire system fell apart across the globe. People experienced job-loss and pay cuts. Both small and large firms had to shut shop. People or businesses with strong cash flows and/or savings were able to tide over.

Because of this, maintaining financial stability is a crucial component of our lives and calls for awareness, knowledge, and action.

I'd say I have been fortunate in this regard. I had no debt or EMIs to be concerned about, I had enough money in savings to cover such unforeseen emergencies. I also had the good fortune of having a consistent income and therefore had no financial worries through the pandemic.

Let's talk about good debt and bad debt while we're talking about debt in general.

Good debt is defined as debt that you incur to purchase an asset that will increase in value over time or will increase your income from such investment. Example: A loan for a home, commercial space, or a business.

Bad debt refers to borrowing money to purchase depreciating assets or assets that won't increase in value or produce revenue. Example: An auto loan or a personal loan.

Businesses take loans for their operations or to grow, expand, and increase their return on investment (ROI). If the company generates enough revenue to cover loan repayments and business expenses, it can survive easily. Problems arise when there is no growth/income, and the company must make debt repayments (principal and interest). This leads to a domino effect that eventually causes businesses to close.

In the past few years, we have witnessed many such businesses shut down due to the non-repayment of business loans. As a result, the entire industrial and banking ecosystem bears the brunt. For instance, if businesses borrow money from banks but cannot repay the loan, they default, which impacts the bank; the bank then writes off the loss, which eventually impacts the economy. We have seen many such examples in the recent times.

On a personal front, there are several ways to consider good debt:

a. An individual borrows money and buys an asset that generates income, for example, a commercial property, from which one can generate rental income and anticipate a gain in the value of the real estate. Even so, we must consider the risks involved, such as the possibility that one may have to pay back the debt out of pocket if one does not receive rental as expected.

b. A person with enough savings takes out a mortgage at a lower interest rate and uses the money saved to invest in equities that produce higher returns, paying off the mortgage and generating a profit.

For example, say, we have savings of X amount, and we can buy a house with that amount. Now, instead of using that money to buy a house, we consider taking a home loan at 5-7% per year and investing this X amount in mutual funds, which usually yields a 10-12% annual return. This covers the house loan interest rate, generates a profit, and gives tax benefits associated with a home loan.

Please note that the rate of interest or return is as on current date, which may change in future. Please calculate and take decisions accordingly.

Both scenarios can be hedged as well. For instance, to be prepared for the unexpected, one can take out a home loan or business loan with insurance. It depends on how wisely the individual handles debt and investments. One should be willing to accept the associated risk and stress.

Coming back to my experiences, I continue to live in a rented house and do not have any immediate intention of buying a house. Any future building or real estate acquisitions would be fully funded out of savings, with no debt. I know it may not be the best decision, but I want to keep it simple and debt-free; this decision is based on my past experiences, and to maintain my sanity!

Being debt-free has benefitted me in many ways:

1. It has allowed me to live a simple, stress-free life without obligations to anyone.

2. I could focus on investing, saving, and increasing my net worth.

3. It has allowed me to ensure the security and preparedness of my family. They need not worry about money.

4. It has helped me control spending.

Emergency Fund

I have been saving money and building an emergency fund over the past few years. It is advisable to have a safety net of six months' expenses set aside for emergencies.

There are several methods of calculating the funds needed:

a. *Emergency fund*: One can save 6-12 months' worth of expenses in savings. For instance, if your monthly spend is X amount, your savings would be *X times 6 or X times 12*. One can make plans based on the need.

b. *Financial stability*: 3-5 years' worth of monthly spending saved will ensure financial stability. For instance, if your monthly spend is X amount, your savings would be *X times 36 months or X times 60 months*. One can then make plans based on the need.

These savings can be invested in liquid funds or a fixed deposit. One should be able to access such funds immediately as and when needed.

Please note above suggestions are based on standard practice recommended by experts. However, you can build your own system or fund which suits you and gives you that comfort.

During the Covid-19 pandemic, we witnessed emergency funds being used when people lost their jobs or had their salaries reduced.

To simplify things, I've set up a 12-month emergency fund. As mentioned, this sum has been invested in liquid assets and fixed deposits. This fund may be utilized for any unforeseen expenses.

I recently had to use my emergency fund because my employer changed, my payments were irregular, and I had a medical emergency. I used my emergency fund to cover my costs. This was quite helpful.

Medical Insurance

For eight years now, I've had my own personal (non-corporate) health insurance (family floater). This insurance now covers all existing illness after the initial three-year waiting period. I also have a significant sum of no-claim bonuses. I independently purchased supplementary insurance for my parents in 2018 which covers pre-existing conditions as well.

My entire family, including my parents, are now protected by two different medical insurance policies.

If one chooses to change jobs or quit job, personal medical insurance is a fallback. Therefore, it is always advisable to obtain private insurance (in addition to corporate insurance) to protect you and your family. This insurance policy should ideally be from a second/different insurance provider, which also serves as a backup in case of a problem with the first insurance provider.

When my employer changed recently, and I was left without corporate insurance, my personal insurance came in handy.

Moving on, in 2021-22, I chose to lower my insured amount for three reasons:

a. I had accrued no claim bonuses.

b. After covid-19, I wanted a higher coverage for the family.

c. There was a top-up option available at a substantially lower price.

After having a thorough discussion with the insurance provider and getting everything in writing, I finally reduced the insured amount by 50% and the premium by 30%+ without affecting the cumulative insured amount.

I used these savings to purchase a top-up medical insurance plan with a significantly bigger covered amount at a much lower premium. This is how top-up plans operate and are considered a better and more affordable choice. One can buy a top-up plan only if there is a base insurance plan.

Let me explain how I did this:

1. In 2021, I cut the insured amount from INR 10L to 5L. As a result, the premium decreased from INR 28,000 to INR 18,000, a 35% drop in the yearly premium.

2. I had accrued INR 6L in bonuses. As a result, I now had INR 11L of coverage (INR 5L of insurance plus INR 6L of bonus).

3. I purchased a top-up plan for an insured amount of INR 1Cr at a premium of INR 12,500 only. I would have otherwise paid INR 70,000 to buy a direct plan of INR 1Cr.

Now I have a medical insurance cover of INR 1.1Cr (main + top-up) at a premium of INR 30,000.

You can see how the same premium might now be used to buy a top-up insurance plan of a considerably higher sum. Although counterintuitive, this is the way top-up plans in insurance work. Of course, the premium amount depends on the age and health factors of the insured. Check for options, evaluate what works for you, talk to an expert, before deciding.

I always choose the yearly payment option to make things as easy as possible. I also consider paying a multi-year premium (two or three years) if I receive a good discount. Since this is a family floater plan, anyone in the family may use it.

So, even if you have a corporate insurance, please consider getting personal insurance. You can start with a lower insured amount. As indicated earlier, this will be useful if one loses workplace/corporate insurance.

Life Insurance

I was inexperienced when it came to investments and insurances. Insurance is sold by agents or advisors as an investment product that offers the advantages of insurance and survival benefits. I consequently purchased numerous endowment insurance policies.

Upon looking closer, I saw that I had been approaching insurance wrongly.

Here is a definition of life insurance:

"Life insurance is a contract between an insurance policy holder and an insurer or assurer, where the insurer promises to pay a designated beneficiary a sum of money upon the death of an insured person." - Wikipedia

As you can see, life insurance does not pay out to the policyholder anything at the end of the policy period but rather pays to the insured's family in the event of the insured's death.

Insurance as an industry is also evolving. Insurance was usually sold as an investment product, which was expensive. But now we have term insurance.

"Term life insurance or term assurance is life insurance that provides coverage at a fixed rate of payments for a limited period, the relevant term." – Wikipedia

Term insurance seems more appropriate given the following advantages:

a. Higher coverage or insurance amount

b. Lower premium

c. Fixed duration, no lock-in

d. Flexibility to change the amount

Finally, I made the decision to cancel all my endowment policies and get a term policy. The insurance premium is affected by several variables, such as insurance coverage, age, and medical history of the insured etc. To keep costs low, it is suggested (by experts or insurance advisors) to start a life insurance policy early and for a long duration (let's say 20 to 30 years). I had to pay a higher premium because I started late and had a pre-existing health condition.

2020–21 saw various adjustments related to life insurance at my end. I did the following:

a. Terminated all my term insurance policies (these had higher insured amounts). I did this for few reasons:

    i. I wanted to save on insurance premium.

    ii. I wanted to split the risk with having insurance policy with single provider.

    iii. I had now enough savings that could take care of my family and no longer needed a greater insured amount. Therefore, it made more sense to purchase term insurance with a lower protected sum.

b. Bought two new term insurance policies from two different insurance companies. I was aware of the possible difficulties families encounter when filing an insurance claim. To mitigate that, I purchased term insurance from two different providers.

c. The total amount insured was equal to 50% of the amount previously covered. As a result, the entire premium was cut in half.

d. Pandemics were also covered by new term insurance policies.

Though I don't need life insurance, as I have a sizeable corpus, and we don't have any liabilities, still, since my family views insurance as security, I'll continue with term insurance, paying a lower premium.

Just to put things in perspective on who should ideally buy an insurance policy – "One should buy a life insurance to protect the dependent family from the potential financial losses that could result if something happened to you. Life insurance provides financial security to the family, helps to pay off debts if any, helps to pay living expenses."

So, if you have enough savings or investments to take care of the family, then you may not need life insurance. Please consult an expert before making any decision.

Once more, for simplicity's sake, I choose to pay premiums annually. I don't use multi-year premium payment options for life insurance, even if it is cheaper. I have also not automated this process. The reason for not paying a multi-year premium or automating this process is to avoid any extra payment in case of an eventuality.

PPF (Public Provident Fund)

I don't have a PF account; I work as a part-time consultant. I opened a PPF account in 2014 and continue to invest in it. Every year, during the first week of April, I put the maximum permissible amount (INR 1.5L a year) into my PPF account and then forget about it.

As many would already know, this is one of the best long-term debt investments, as the interest rate fixed by the Government and is revised every year. The best part is that the interest we earn is tax-free.

When the interest payment is made by the government to my PPF account at the end of each fiscal year, compound interest is visible in action. Watching the money grow without any effort is quite satisfying.

This investment will continue to grow at its own pace and requires no attention, except once a year when money needs to be deposited into the PPF account.

To simplify this further, I invest the total permissible amount during the first week of the start of the fiscal year. I have also automated this process, transferring the money from my savings account to my PPF account.

The great paradox of this remarkable age is that the more complex the world around us becomes, the more simplicity we must seek in order to realize our financial goals. Simplicity, indeed, is the master key to financial success.

– Jack Bogle

Bank Accounts and Credit Card

I still have one credit card and one savings account. For simplicity of usage and maintenance, they are both from the same bank.

Most of my transactions are made with a debit card or UPI both are connected to the same savings account. I pay all bills on time, including rent, electricity, credit card, and other utility bills. These payments are generally automated. Likewise, all my investments are automated.

Monthly expenses are covered by the money left over after payments and investments. I don't hold onto any extra money.

I use the credit card mindfully. I ensure payments in full every month. Additionally, I use credit cards at airport lounges and for reward points. It also maintains my credit rating.

I pay credit card bills manually after carefully reviewing statements for expenses I have made. This enables me to track my spending and, if necessary, take corrective action.

"Happiness is not fulfilling every pleasure or getting every outcome you desire. Happiness is being able to enjoy life with a peaceful mind that is not constantly craving for more. It is the inner peace that comes with embracing change."

– Yung Pueblo

Manage Spending

When I was younger, my parents would hand me a list of groceries that needed to be bought from the nearby grocery store. Back then, there were no supermarkets. I would just go out and purchase the things on that list. Nothing more, nothing less. Life was so structured. We knew exactly what to buy and how much to buy.

Nowadays, we visit supermarkets, purchase more items than we need, and overspend.

Tracking expenses is the first step in managing them. This will enable us to understand our purchasing habits and welcome simplicity in our lives.

To keep track of expenses and spending, most people use spreadsheets. I use Google Sheets so that I can access it from anywhere. Find a tool that meets your needs and is simple to use. Please don't make this process too difficult. Ensure sustainability and simplicity.

To track, you may also consider opening a second bank account where you deposit a certain amount for monthly expenses and use that account solely for this purpose. This is an effective way of tracking monthly expenses. One can also apply for a second credit card to be used for regular monthly expenses only.

Most of my recurring payments are listed (monthly and yearly). This gives me the visibility of my fixed expenses. Monthly recurring expenses include rent, phone, internet, grocery, fuel, electricity, water, subscriptions, etc.

Some of the yearly expenses could be insurance premiums, school fees, property tax, subscriptions, etc. There are always incidental expenses that cannot be foreseen and are unplanned, like medical, shopping, etc. It's a good idea to keep a buffer for such expenses.

Let's look at the graphs below to gain a better understanding of our spending patterns or behaviours:

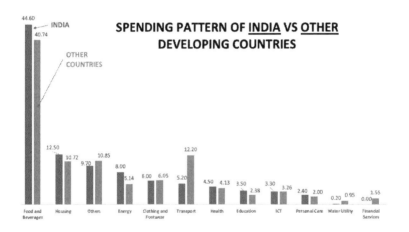

Sector	India %	Other Countries %
Food and Beverages	44.60	40.74
Housing	12.50	10.72
Others	9.70	10.85
Energy	8.00	5.14
Clothing and Footwear	6.00	6.05
Transport	5.20	12.20
Health	4.50	4.13
Education	3.50	2.38
ICT	3.30	3.26
Personal Care	2.40	2.00
Water Utility	0.20	0.95
Financial Services	0.00	1.55
	100	100

80%+ goes here

73%+ goes here

Source: https://getmoneyrich.com/consumer-spending/

You can check the source, where author Mani has done some detailed analysis.

Let's examine the top 5 spending categories. We spend 40-45% of our budget on *food and beverages*. This is where most of our money is spent.

Tracking will help to find such patterns and take corrective action when needed. If left untracked, we won't know where the bulk of our spending lies.

Businesses keep balance sheet and track every penny. The same should be done by individuals. Planning will be more effective when we understand where the money is coming from and where it is going.

As mentioned, I make all recurring payments and investments, at the beginning of each month itself. I follow this as a process, which has been greatly automated. As a result, things are simplified.

After payments and investments, we are left with a limited amount of money for monthly expenses. This process keeps us on track. Any unexpected additional expense can be managed out of the emergency fund, which should be replenished in the next month.

Spending habits can be controlled with the help of minimalism and essentialism. It also helps in altering consumption habits. I purchase services/products only when essential. With simple living, I prevent accumulation. Some of the rules I follow:

1. Defer the buying decision so we buy only what is essential. This is a tried and tested practice. By doing this, impulsive decisions are avoided.

2. For something new to enter, something old must go out.

3. Buy vs rent. Almost everything is available for rent today. Evaluate if it is better to rent or to buy.

Nick Maggiulli, the creator of "Of Dollars And Data" and the Chief Operating Officer at Ritholtz Wealth Management, suggested the 2x rule, which essentially means making an equal amount of investment for every expense. For instance, if you want to spend X dollars on a pair of shoes, or a watch, or a phone, you should also invest an equal amount. You know that you must budget for investing an equal amount each time you plan to spend that money. This discipline will not only make you think twice before spending but also help you save and invest if you eventually decide to spend.

Debt and excessive spending can make you fragile. To live a simpler life, you must identify your weak points and take steps to eliminate them.

On the other hand, entrepreneur Ramit Sethi writes in his book *I Will Teach You to Be Rich,* that after taking care of your assets and savings, you should be able to spend your money guilt-free. Take that vacation, purchase a business class ticket, purchase the pricey clothing you have always desired, and enjoy that cup of coffee. We work to enjoy a few things in life, so why work if we can't even use what we get paid for? Maybe he has a point too, but with "conditions apply".

Too many people spend money they haven't earned, to buy things they don't want, to impress people they don't like.

– Will Smith

Income Generation

Controlling our spending habits has its limits. To a certain extent, we can reduce or regulate our expenditure; after that, nothing can be done. Spending cannot go to zero.

We must prioritise boosting our income while reducing our spending. Increased money can result in two things:

a. Our expenditure rises along with our income. Typically, this is what occurs. With increased income, we now desire more, bigger, and better things, also as a result of lifestyle changes, and newer spending patterns.

b. Although our income rises, our spending does not. This enhances the odds of saving and investing more. This is the ideal situation to be in.

Nick Maggiulli gives two great suggestions in his book *Just Keep Buying*

i. Savings have a limitation, but income has no limitations. So focus more on income generation.

ii. 2x rule – As discussed before, when you want to spend on something expensive, ensure you invest an equal amount in stocks or any other income-generating instrument.

The inflation rate is an additional consideration while generating revenue and estimating consumption. The amount spent on the same object rises with inflation. To pay for that, one must produce greater income, to handle inflation.

It is essential to create multiple sources or streams of income. They help in:

a. Creating backup if one source is affected

b. More income results in more savings and investments

c. More income allows for freer spending

Over time, the living expense has gone up. According to statistics, prices have increased faster than income growth. As a result, we can spend less of our income on purchases. Consider the price of real estate. An average person struggles to afford it. Consequently, having several sources of income and generating greater money has become essential.

Long-term passive income creation should be prioritised in addition to having active income streams. The main goal of the FIRE (financial independence and early retirement) journey is to have passive income. True financial independence entails not having to worry about money. Rather than working for money, one should have money working for them.

To simplify life, I have been able to create multiple sources of income over the years:

a. Active income from consulting

b. Active income from trading

c. Passive income from dividends

d. Passive income from rentals

e. Passive income as interests from deposits

f. Passive income from the stock market

Active income is income received from a job or business venture that you actively participate in. Examples of active income include wages, salaries, bonuses, commissions, tips, and net earnings from self-employment.

Passive income is earnings derived from a rental property, limited partnership, or another enterprise in which a person is not actively involved.

In this digital age, there are many possibilities and ways to establish multiple income streams, for example, content creation, gig work, image or video creation/editing etc. To find areas of personal interest that will create revenue, one must look into one's strength areas and discover one's abilities, interests, and passions.

If you are working for an organization full-time, then you need to check the possibility of engaging in moonlighting, as it is not acceptable by many organizations. Having multiple income streams in such cases becomes difficult or limited. So, find the options available for you and take steps towards that.

As you age, luxury is not about owning a lot of stuff; it is about not having deadlines, it is about feeling unhurried, it is about slowing down and not being answerable to anyone while doing so.

– Vishal Khandelwal

Investments

Investing is a critical action and is a true game changer. Over the last few years, especially after publishing my first book, my focus has been on building my corpus of funds. Now I think it has reached a reasonable size and should possibly take care of my family and me for the rest of our lives.

I invest about 70-80% of my annual income. This is possible, as I have reached a stage where I can limit my expenses and invest the rest of them. This may not be possible at the start of a career. So, try to save maximum and increase this saving every year.

My primary investment goal is to protect capital and to take advantage of market cycles and the power of compounding. I have a long way to go before I realize and take advantage of the true power of compounding. This is because I started saving and investing very late in life. Regardless of your position or compensation, it is imperative to get started as early as possible. Start modestly and expand from there. It is all about realizing the importance of investing and starting early.

The best time to start investing is now! Earlier, the better. I did not start early and missed the opportunity. But it is never too late. Start today!

Thanks to my friend and advisor, Samrat, who has been helping me with money management and constantly educating me.

My investments consist largely of mutual funds and real estate. Most of it is invested in balanced mutual funds, which include debt and equity. Even if the return is less than expected, the goal is to protect the capital. I also participate in a systemic investment plan (SIP).

I have investments in two professionally managed, all-equity funds besides the MFs. These investments are based on momentum strategies.

Additionally, I have invested in real estate investment trusts (REITs), which pay quarterly dividends. They seem to have great potential to grow and provide consistent income.

Most of these investments are automated, with dividends directly being deposited into my bank account and monthly SIPs leaving my account on autopilot.

My emergency funds are in FDs (fixed deposits) and liquid funds.

I stay away from Bonds, cryptocurrencies, non-fungible tokens (NFTs), alternative investment funds (AIFs), soulbound tokens (SBTs), commodities, peer-to-peer lending, discount invoicing, etc. I don't invest in them because either I don't understand them, or I am not comfortable dealing with high volatility, or they are not regulated. That is the choice I made. You may have a different viewpoint and may consider investing in them after evaluating the risks involved.

I am attempting to keep my investments simple, safe, regulated, and something that I can manage on my own.

People who do not have the time and skills can start with mutual funds. Others who have an interest and can spend time learning more about investments and can explore many investment options. There are many Fintech platforms today that will facilitate these investments. Talk to an expert to get some advice if required, even if it means paying for such advice. Plenty of relevant content is available on the internet. Learn about the subject and stay invested.

One straightforward investment strategy is to invest in Index funds.

Index funds are mutual funds or exchange-traded funds (ETFs) whose portfolio mirrors that of a designated index, aiming to match its performance. Over the long term, index funds have generally outperformed other types of mutual funds. Other benefits of index funds include low fees, tax advantages (they generate less taxable income), and low risk (since they're highly diversified).

If you notice, the very nature of an index is to go up, so investing in an index is a sure-shot profit. There are also dips, which could be excellent opportunities to buy.

Again, please do your own research or talk to an expert before making any investment decision. It is your money, and you are responsible for it.

Finance and investment have been an area of interest ever since I realized their importance in becoming debt-free and, therefore, simplifying life. I have done plenty of reading on finance and investments, trying to learn from others about their experience, how they manage their money, and their investment philosophy.

A common trait shared by many of these great investors is that they have kept their investment approach relatively straightforward and simple. Successful investors don't aim to time or outperform the market. Instead, they have their strategies to which they adhere to consistently. They are not competing to show that they are the best or better than someone.

I continue to trade. I love the concept of trading. However, it requires a lot of discipline and is not for everyone. *More on trading in the next chapter.*

I think everybody should get rich and famous and do everything they ever dreamed of so they can see that it's not the answer.

— Jim Carrey

Children's Education and Marriage Fund

I am very clear on this subject. I will cover the cost of primary education of both my daughters. They must sponsor their fees for professional courses (Medical, Engineering, Masters, or any other course of their interest), get employed, and pay the resultant EMIs.

Similarly, they must find their partners and sponsor their weddings.

Enough

Unless we know when to slow down, halt, or until we realize when it is enough, life becomes a vicious cycle.

In the modern world, we are constantly rushing without knowing where we're headed. Even if we reach our goal, we tend to keep moving the goalposts, which continue till the end of life.

For most of us, the struggle seems to be a never-ending story. We have less needs and objectives before we start making money. After we accomplish something, we seem to require more and more. Our efforts to satiate our increasing desires never seem to stop growing.

Let's use money as an example. When we earn a particular amount, we plan our lives according to that. We strive for better lifestyles as our income rises. As we adjust to the new way of living, we exert more effort to keep it up, and the cycle repeats. The worst scenario is when people borrow money to support a certain lavish lifestyle.

Consider some additional examples: We constantly desire to purchase more expensive designer clothing, larger homes, and expensive cars. This is a never-ending search for more. There is always an alternative that is bigger, better, and more expensive. Our identity is reduced to that of being a consumer. We keep accumulating, thereby complicating our lives.

The urge to replicate or adapt to what one sees on social media has increased this phenomenon because it has a psychological effect and puts pressure on people to earn more and spend more. People are social creatures who like to impress others. As we begin to imitate others, we stop paying attention to our own thoughts and life. We begin to live for others.

Imagine the barrage of advertisements that make you feel inferior if you did not purchase the goods they are promoting. Often, the cost of marketing and advertising is higher for businesses than the price of the original product itself.

For most of us, money-making has become the sole purpose in life, and we don't know when to say 'enough' as we have never learned to say enough.

For instance, every company in the world has growth goals that they follow year after year. They never stop or slow down. Most of us work for some type of company or organization, either as employees, employers, or gig workers; we all are aware that the goals are raised every year, and we are expected to work towards those higher goals. Have you ever come across a company that would say, "Enough, we don't want to grow further, and we are pleased with what we have and would focus on maintaining it or maybe even cutting it down"? The answer is - probably not. That is the nature of any business and individuals who run businesses.

We must identify where we stand in the larger scheme of things and what we want to achieve and when is enough for us.

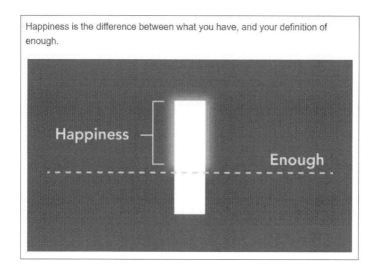

I have been trying to simplify life by defining what is enough for me. I took a pay cut for reduced work hours a few years ago. I could make that choice because I knew what was enough for me, wanted freedom and more time with family, friends, and children. Of course, this wouldn't have been possible without the support of my boss and the organization.

A lot depends on what you want from life and what your life goals are. One must draw a line somewhere; else life will be an endless endeavor.

Saying "enough" in today's culture is extremely challenging because everyone is vying for "more" - more money, more possessions, more ego, more power, more attention, more fame, and more of everything. The word "enough" may come across as a demotivating or limiting term.

Well, that's a choice one makes. I made my choice. You make yours.

There are two ways to get enough: One is to continue to accumulate more and more. The other is to desire less.

– G.K. Chesterton

Chapter 2
Trading

I want to talk more about my trading (stocks, shares, futures, and options) journey in this chapter, including how I got started, the mistakes I made, the ups and downs, and the emotional rollercoaster the stock market can be.

I also understood that my experience was not unusual and, in fact, is quite typical of most traders. Undoubtedly, many of us have experienced a similar journey.

I started my investment journey sometime in 2014-15 when I was looking at the equity market seriously. Let's examine each of these stages in greater detail.

Phase 1:

It came about by chance. I wanted to buy life insurance. My bank advised I look at a couple of unit-linked life insurance products during one of those conversations. I decided to discuss this with my bank as I had savings account with the same bank and reasoned it would be simpler to transact with them.

The bank representative visited me to explain the different options. I relied on the representative to provide me with all the necessary information to decide, as I was not an expert in this area.

The representative also advised me to consider mutual funds for a larger return on the investment during one such conversation. Even though I had no interest in the stock market, I decided to at least take the information. He succeeded in persuading me to invest in four different mutual funds after multiple discussions.

I had the convenience of investing and withdrawing money with a single login to access my savings and mutual fund accounts. I was enthusiastic as I was attempting something new.

As soon as I began investing in mutual funds, I also began discussing various investing options with friends. Talking about money with family and friends is not very common. A few people who participated in these discussions with me indicated how they invested in stock directly and took home reasonable returns without depending on anyone. I began to enquire because I was inquisitive. Looking back, I felt like I was in a hurry to learn quickly and act.

Phase 2:

I needed to register for a Demat account to invest in equities. Contacting my bank, which also offered a Demat account and trading desk, was a simpler and faster choice.

I opened a Demat account immediately. The same bank had my salary account, mutual fund account, and now the Demat account.

Though I opened the Demat account, I still did not know how to invest or which stocks to buy. So, I did the next best thing – I asked my friends. A few gave tips; some suggested reading financial journals and following recommendations. I started investing small amounts based on these tips and began to buy and sell stocks. This is how I started my stock market journey. The period of learning continued.

Phase 3:

On one of those days, my good old pal Robin called to ask whether I would like to join him in attending an introduction to the trading class. I responded 'yes' because I was in that frame of mind.

"When you want something, the whole universe conspires to make it happen." - Paulo Coelho

We went to the introductory class with Vaibhav Kale, which was an amazing session. I was introduced to a whole new world and perspective on the stock market and trading. It opened my mind to a promising and encouraging field. Since I was looking for an alternative source of income, this option looked good. We signed up for his two-day program. With Vaibhav, we attended two more programs where we learned about technical analysis, trading, equities, options, and futures.

This is how my trading journey began.

Phase 4:

Robin and I had met Ankit during one of these programs. He had a better grasp of trading. I was still having trouble grasping the fundamentals. We grew close and had lengthy conversations about trading. One day, he brought up the mentor program for traders. I've always had a lot of regard for mentors and coaches.

Ankit and I spoke to Vishal Malkan. After many rounds of discussion, we eventually enrolled to the mentor program. It was a significant decision, as it was an expensive program. We considered this as an alternative career for us.

Together, Vishal and Meghna Malkan elevated us completely to a new level. A well-designed curriculum with components devoted to mindset, homework, reading exercises, support, techniques, mastermind meetings, and many other elements. We were doing well.

Phase 5:

Before completing our foundational curriculum, we were not permitted to trade.

We were finally given the green light to trade after few months of intensive training. We were told to begin modestly. Equities were listed first, followed by futures and options.

We were instructed to proceed slowly and steadily, using one or two techniques at a time with less equity or just one lot of futures.

Despite all this training and instructions, I had already begun to break the rules intentionally or unintentionally. I wanted to get things done quickly and was aggressive, impatient, and curious.

When I would talk to my mentors about my transactions, they would correct me and tell me to take things gradually. Nonetheless, I became easily distracted and continued to trade aggressively, making mistakes, and losing money.

When you hear about other people's successes while you are struggling, it starts to hurt. Comparing oneself to others gradually turned into a major obstacle and disrupted the entire learning process. Instead of doing as we were told, I asked others about their effective techniques.

There is a proverb that goes, "One feels delighted about another person's failure and sad about another person's success." Additionally, this is when self-doubt begins to creep in.

Without my knowledge, I had entered a black hole.

Phase 6:

Over the following few years, I focused on understanding my feelings and reactions.

Every time I vowed to adhere to guidelines rigorously, I would falter and breach them during the weak moments, disrupting the entire strategy and, in the process, affecting my trading record (hits, wins, misses and probability, etc.). This persisted for a while. This is when I began reading and studying others' strategies because I could not trade profitably. I started searching for any strategy that would yield better results while ignoring that trading was mostly a mental game.

I would attend more classes with other trainers and hope to learn something new and be a successful trader. I assumed strategy was everything.

This quest for learning led to a few more trainers and many more strategies. Not that I was short of systems or strategies, but my need to find a surefire technique kept me searching for more.

I played around with futures, options, and stocks. Since the results were slow, I was not really excited by stocks. I, therefore, invested more time in futures and options. I experimented with positional trading, swing trading, and day trading. I put every plan to the test. I switched from one system to another in the hope of earning consistently. I could not wait and lacked the patience to stick with one strategy. I spent most of my time in front of the screen. Without realizing it, it was turning this into an addiction. Unconsciously and soon enough, this began to add to my stress. Although there was no financial pressure, the fact that I was failing consistently became an ego issue, leading me to revenge trade at times.

I would discuss trading strategies with friends. Everyone now used their own technique and method for trading. You can find thousands of professionals, trainers, and traders explaining their trading methods and tactics on the internet. In an effort to study everything there is to know, I started jumping from one friend to another, one link to another, and one video to another, hoping to find the holy grail that would make me a good trader one day.

Because trading allowed me to earn unlimited income and enjoy the time freedom I had always desired, it captivated me.

Don't reinvent the wheel, Vishal would constantly advise; "I've already done the research, backtesting, and mistakes. Use the approach exactly as it is". Additionally, he said, "It's 80% mindset and 20% strategy." Whether it be the strategy or execution, he repeatedly insisted that we keep things simple.

Although I always kept his advice in mind, I was not acting on it because my heart and thoughts were out of alignment. I kept looking for that one holy grail that would bring the money. Perhaps I am one of those people who prefer to make mistakes on my own dime rather than learn from others' experiences. It was proving to be incredibly pricey.

For some reason, I was in a hurry. By the time I realized this, I had already spent a few years and lot of money looking for that holy grail. I am not sure why I did not stop or seek help. I was one of the best students but failed to make it big. Maybe I had the luxury of a monthly income, which allowed me to experiment.

The following three to four years went by before I grew weary and declared that I could no longer carry-on trading in this manner. It cannot be so difficult, and it should be simple, I said to myself. I did not sign up for trading to make my life complicated.

It was time to slow down and simplify trading and my life.

Phase 7:

I finally realized that trading was not only about strategy anymore. It was about time, patience, discipline, and following the rules – it was more about the mind.

I also understood that, when used consistently, even a straightforward approach like moving average would produce excellent results.

It was time to slow down and simplify. I decided to use two simple strategies and reduced quantity for trading.

I'll stick with this approach, adhere to guidelines, exercise restraint, and be patient. I feel at peace when using simple strategies, following the rules, and keeping the risk minimal.

The best part of this journey is that I did not quit. I had, without realizing it, complicated a simple process. Profit or loss, success or failure, I kept going, never gave up, and was always in the market. Now only time will tell if I'll be a profitable trader.

I no longer trade options; I only trade futures now. I follow the trend and momentum strategies. This seems to suit my temperament.

Additionally, I intend to take a break from trading and concentrate on investing until I have brought my investments up to a specific level and then resume trading.

No person can play the market all the time and win. There are times when you should be completely out of the market, for emotional as well as economic reasons.

– Jesse Livermore

How I simplified my trading

1. Now, I use only two technical indicators – Moving average and relative strength index (RSI).

2. Use only one indicator for any trade. Adding multiple indicators makes it confusing, contradicting at times, and decision-making becomes difficult.

3. Follow a simple process with discipline on the daily or weekly chart.

4. Trade only in futures. No options trading till I gain more experience.

5. No more screen gazing all the time. A simple process with consistency, spending only 15-20 minutes a day.

6. Trade in not more than three stocks at any time. I may increase the lot size but stick to only 2-3 stocks/positions.

7. No timing the market or wondering why the market behaves in a certain way.

8. No watching the news or following anyone on social media, so I don't get influenced by anyone. I have also stopped discussing the market with anyone.

Trading can be run as a business in two ways:

1. Solo: Trade without any external support or manpower. Many successful traders run this business solo for themselves and their clients.

2. Team: Build a team that follows pre-defined rules and processes and manages money.

There are pros and cons to both. One can decide what works best for them. I like to go solo.

When I entered the stock market, I did not realize how deep it could go. There are thousands of trainers, books, YouTube videos, and courses. One can feel lost listening to too many opinions in the pursuit of mastering the skill. It can take a lifetime, and you may still feel that there is more to learn. I never thought I would go so deep. I have spent many years trying to learn the art of trading and investment and still feel lost.

During training, every system and strategy shown on the screen seems profitable. We usually learn a lot more from personal experiences than from lessons in the classroom.

Accepting that we cannot expect unrealistic returns and accepting the fact that the typical return is usually between 15% and 20% in a year is also crucial. We will be at ease and be able to become successful traders if we accept this fact.

If you don't understand trading or it is not something you like or enjoy doing, then accept it, and be OK to give your money to experts who can manage it. Do your due diligence before investing, as, ultimately, it is your money.

As William Green, author of the book 'Richer, Wiser, Happier' says, "I'm smart enough to know that I need to outsource it. I can see the difference between them (wise and experienced investors) and me. And so, one of the practical revelations that I got from working on the book was just to say, I'm not them, and I don't have their wiring,

I don't have their temperament. I'm not as obsessed with this stuff as they are. And so, I should give my money to people who are better wired for this game."

The best-case scenario is to have our money make more money for us. Once the money is out of the focus area, we can focus on other things in life. If we spend 15+ hours a day working for money for our entire life, where is the time for anything else?

You may spend your entire adult life saving for your kids, and they may not even want anything from you. Pointless goals sometimes.

— Alok Jain (weekendinvesting.com)

Chapter 3
Health

*H*ealth is wealth. Period.

Covid-19 taught us this very well.

I pondered my future steps after dropping almost 20 kgs through altered eating and activity routines. It should have been simple from there to keep going and maintain the status quo.

The monkey mind, however, kept asking for the *next goal*. I decided to combine outdoor exercise with the gym since I was getting bored at the gym. Eventually, my gym membership expired, and I did not renew it. I decided to combine yoga with outdoor walking now. I constantly made changes in the routine to avoid boredom.

Things started to change gradually. Food preferences also began to change. Everything I had previously avoided began to beckon to me once more.

I consulted my brother. He mentioned that fitness is 80% food and 20% exercise. The whole system should be sustainable even when we are not well or not in a position to exercise.

Eating Habits

So, I now started focusing on food. It involved both quality, quantity of food, and the eating time. My goal was to maintain my weight without exercise for six months. I successfully managed my weight with a fluctuation of 1-2 kgs for this period. Six months became a year without physical exercise.

I gradually included morning walks and various exercises into my routine. Before we knew it, we were hit by Covid-19, and life went for a toss.

I tried talking to the experts. Eating a calculated quantity of food by measurement did not work for me. It complicated the eating process. Simple homemade cooked food was good enough. I had some tests done to identify food allergies to avoid such foods. The diet plan was to eat good homemade food in lesser quantities. I did not need more. In fact, after a few days, my body couldn't take more food than was needed. This general practice simplified my life.

I enjoy watching YouTube food channels, especially those that feature street food. I observed that we had complicated our eating habits over time. We mix anything with everything as long it tastes good. I'm hesitant even to attempt this kind of food.

According to my brother (a naturopath) and several other doctors, most of our health issues are stomach/gut related. Most health problems can be avoided or cured by eating correctly.

Simplify food. Eat simple and staple food. Eat food that has been eaten over generations in the region we stay in. Eat seasonal, regional fruits and vegetables. Do not mix many ingredients.

Study Ayurveda to understand how mixing food can be toxic to the body. Such toxic food may not have an immediate impact on the body, but constant abuse of our body can have a severe and sometimes irreversible, irreparable impact.

The diet programs I tried did not work for me. I attempted to simplify my dietary habits. I would:

a. Eat when hungry

b. Eat what the body needs

c. Eat slowly and consciously

d. Stop when the body has had enough

Sleeping Habits

My awareness of sleeping habits has improved lately. Doctors are now recommending better sleeping habits for overall wellness. Sleeping early and getting up early is getting back into vogue. I have been eating and sleeping early for a few years now, and they really help. I don't need an alarm. My body clock is now tuned to getting up early.

Digital Habits (looking at/working on electronic screens of any kind)

Everyone is talking about digital well-being. Doctors suggest keeping the usage of electronic screens to a minimum. Many adults and kids are addicted to phones/digital devices to the point where they cannot imagine life without them. For many, that is life. There has been an increase in crime, murders, suicides, stress, and mental issues as a result of uncontrolled usage of electronic devices. Repeated studies seem to have established a correlation between these two. The list goes on and on, but you get the point.

Finding activities that don't require these devices, such as cooking, spending time with family and friends, gardening, cleaning the house, going for a stroll, window shopping, or even reading a book (not on Kindle or another e-reading device), is the most effective method of dealing with digital addiction. Reading books has helped me stay away from digital devices.

According to research, the body experiences significant stress because of increased screen time and the resulting information consumption. Eyes are glued to screens, and the mind is preoccupied with consuming and processing information for very long periods of time. This affects how our body functions.

I had the experience of being cut off from technology and not using a device for three to four consecutive days for the first time in recent years when I went out on a group mountain trek. Since we did not have any signal, we never looked at our phones; however, we had beautiful nature, fellow trekkers to converse with and engage in group activities, and a few dogs and horses who accompanied us. Life looked so simple, fresh, and enriching. I was in awe of that experience. I still treasure that memory.

When I got back from that trek, my daily screen usage went back to my usual high levels. Not surprisingly, after a few days, I began to feel the stress again, had a heavy head, and had trouble sleeping. This experience only confirmed the effects of prolonged screen usage and information consumption.

Amongst other things, this could explain why today's kids tend to be so aggressive, restless, volatile, and irritable.

How I manage my digital life now:

1. I use a PC for most of my work.

2. I use the mobile phone mainly for calling and avoid using it for any other purposes or unless I am traveling and don't have access to a PC.

3. I use only a few apps, depending on the requirement.

4. At one point, I was trying to use tools to block me from using digital devices/apps. Imagine using an app on your mobile phone to avoid using another. Well, this did not work for me. I realized that if I have to avoid screen time, I must find a non-digital substitute. I got back to reading physical books rather than on Kindle. I now prefer to spend time with physical objects or with people.

There are various things we can do to manage our health. Try different things to find what works for you. Consult experts if required. But keep it simple.

This is how I simplified things:

1. Eat simple, staple food.

2. Consume food prepared at home with love and positive energy.

3. Dining with loved ones.

4. Eat slowly and savor your food.

5. Eat with hands, let the tongue tell what to eat, let the stomach tell how much to eat, and let the body decide what it likes and how it feels.

6. Eat fresh, organic (if possible), seasonal and local food.

7. Eat early. If you start early, then you can end early - breakfast before 8 am, lunch before 1 pm, and dinner before 6 or 7 pm.

8. You can also practice intermittent fasting or eat two meals a day. However, always aim at simplicity in your eating habits.

9. Go to bed early and let the body determine the wake-up time. You will gradually see changes if you practice this for a few days. Frankly, when my body gets enough sleep, I even get up at 3 or 4 am, and still feel fresh and energetic. But it is very important that I get some rest. I get disturbed if I don't get enough sleep. It takes me at least a week to get back to normalcy. This is the way my body is tuned. When I was much younger, I could stay up all night; now, I simply cannot. My body tells me that this is enough, and it will not be able to withstand any more atrocities.

10. Get food allergy tests done to find food suitable for your body. This can eliminate plenty of problems.

11. Go outdoors for a run or a walk. Although daily discipline and routine are preferable, don't worry if you miss the routine occasionally. Implement it at your own pace. Keep it simple.

12. Gyms cost money. Yoga, body weight exercises, running, and walking are free alternatives for staying fit.

Life is really simple, but we insist on making it complicated.

– Confucious

Chapter 4

Work

I had no idea what I was getting into when I started my work life. This happened to me in the natural course of things, as it would for most people.

Being born, getting educated, getting a job, marriage, procreation, raising children, retirement, senility, and death. This is the normal human lifecycle. And between these phases, if you get a chance, you may want to consider doing things you like – following your passion and doing things you love.

We appear to be working all the time. Working was supposed to be a small part of our life for survival, but that no longer seems to be the case.

Usually, getting up early and getting ready to leave for work takes two or three hours, then the commute takes another hour or two. Work takes nine or ten hours, and the commute back home is another one or two hours. You reach home and then unwind for some time. After that, you get ready for household chores which take another hour or two. In this way, we work for a total of 15-16 hours per day. Add another eight hours of sleep, and we are done with a 24-hour cycle.

This is the typical life for most of us. This leaves no time for anything else. We seem to sacrifice sleep to accommodate more work. We are living to work rather than working to live. I did this as well for a long time, and it did hurt me deeply.

Shut down that email server, and you will know where we spend most of our time at work. When emails don't work, I've witnessed staff freaking out and becoming anxious. Some even claim they cannot work without access to email. We appear to spend most of our time reading and replying to emails.

It is quite normal to anticipate a prompt reply to emails; failing to do so is seen as being impolite or lazy. Add to that the instant messaging tools. In this way, we are primed to be accessible and responsive across various communication platforms, including emails, MS Teams, Zoom, Slack, WhatsApp, and SMS, among others. Life seems to revolve around these tools.

When I became aware of how entangled I was in these tools, I began looking for other tools to govern or regulate this behavior on both PC and mobile devices. Naturally, this proved to be highly ineffective. It necessitates discipline and self-control.

Around 2014, I reduced my work to three days a week. I'm very grateful to my boss for approving this arrangement. Back then, flexi-work wasn't common. Six years later, I changed from working three days a week to a half-day each day to meet business needs.

I feel my generation has needlessly complicated their lives. The next generation seems aware of these difficulties and is more balanced in their approach to work and life.

I also think many of us are just addicted to work. We get our high from working long hours. For many, work is life, and that's the personal choice they make. Not everyone would like to live like this. Many are looking for more balance in life, but that seems impossible unless the whole ecosystem changes.

In an effort to do many activities and do them quickly, we have, without realizing it, complicated our lives. We set ourselves aggressive goals and end up racing against the clock for the rest of our lives. Some of us have set short-term goals but keep moving the goalposts randomly. It appears like there is no end to these desires. We don't seem to stop, ever. Life has become so mechanical.

We have gotten addicted to our paycheques, and it is nearly impossible to think of a life without this regular salary or income.

Not that I dislike working. Since I enjoy my line of work, I frequently put in long hours. I am sure you will also agree that when work gets engaging, we lose the sense of time and get deeply involved.

Steps I took to simplify my work life:

1. I started with a three-day workweek arrangement with my employer. Then I shifted to a half-day of work every day of the week (Monday to Friday).

2. Work from home: Most of my work gets done remotely. I have been working from home for a few years now. My daily commute to work and back would last for 3-4 hours; I thought I could spend this time productively by working from home. My boss understood this and accepted my work-from-home regime. WFH was not a standard practice back then. However, Covid came along and changed the whole perspective, and WFH became a new normal and acceptable practice. I acknowledge that this may not be an option for everyone.

3. Better email management

   a. I created a separate folder for Cc emails and set a rule to move my emails from Inbox to Cc whenever my name is mentioned in the Cc field. Emails with Cc are only for my information and don't require immediate attention or action. I check them a couple of times during the day and make sure all emails are attended to.

   b. I request politely that I not be included in emails that don't require any action from my end. Attending to each email takes away a lot of time, and I have a habit of giving equal attention to all emails and messages. So, it is better not to be a part of emails that do not require my attention.

   c. I removed new email notifications as this is a huge distraction. Try to disable this and see if it helps in improving your productivity. I have disabled all notifications – both on PC and mobile.

d. Close the email client (Microsoft Outlook in my case). We invariably keep checking emails if Outlook is open. I keep Outlook closed most of the time. I open it periodically to check my Inbox (not Cc) and respond or add something to my task list if an action is required. This helps me focus on my tasks when I am not checking emails.

e. Respond to emails only when urgent or requires immediate attention, which does not take much time. Other emails that are not urgent and require more extended responses can be attended to later.

4. Meetings: We spend a lot of time attending meetings. The task list piles up, and then, we try to figure out how to complete pending tasks. Now we start compromising on sleep and personal time to complete the pending tasks. I was getting overwhelmed with meetings, so I took a few steps to simplify things:

a. I make a conscious effort to have not more than 2-3 meetings a day.

b. The meeting duration ideally should not be more than 30 minutes. There are a few mandatory meetings that last longer than 30 minutes, and that cannot be avoided. But I try to keep all other meetings short.

c. If I get a meeting invite, I check with the sender if my presence is required or if any action is required from my end. This helps me understand if I am required on the call as a participant or just an observer. If not necessary, I avoid the call or meeting.

5. Multi-tasking: This is counter-productive. A few people do it so often that they get used to it and start liking it. I used to multitask as well. But now, I like to do one thing at a time with complete focus and attention. I noticed that my overall productivity decreases when I multitask, and I also get highly stressed. Stress starts affecting my sleep as my mind is occupied and is not at peace, and then it starts affecting my overall health. So, I understood that I must now find some balance between my own life and work.

The world has started discussing and emphasizing workplace mental health, and organizations are adapting their work cultures to align with this.

Many organizations are open to new ideas like four days of the work week, three days of work from the office and two from home, 4-6 hours a day of work, and various such combinations.

6. Work less: I came to the realisation somewhere along the way that I was so occupied with my daily tasks that I had no time to go exploring. When we work less, we have more time for socialising, reading, learning, acquiring fresh insights, and engaging in new activities. Working less results in more time being spent on activities other than routine work. We no longer understand what "doing nothing" entails. Being busy has become a trend that we flaunt with pride. Too much work can be damaging to our mental and physical health. Regardless of whether we are passionate about our jobs or not, we are supposed to work to live, not just live to work.

We are here to live. Not to earn, not to stress, not to prove, not even to please. Just to live.

– Natasha Helwig

Chapter 5

Life and Everything Else

*L*ife has gotten complicated, or perhaps I should say we have complicated our own lives. If we have complicated it, then we should be able to untangle and simplify it as well.

Visualize our life in a city where everyone is competing and running. We don't seem to have time for ourselves, let alone time for others. We work all week for the employer, then on the weekends, we work for ourselves. There is not a moment of rest or empty space.

In today's time, visiting or meeting someone requires a great level of planning and effort. We have to ensure their availability, willingness to host, and a long commute for a relatively short visit. This takes up the whole day. But who has so much time? So, we end up not visiting.

Gone are the days when we visited our relatives during holidays for a few days or weeks. Kids would enjoy themselves in the company of other relatives/cousins. When was the last we did this in recent times? We wouldn't have. No one has so much time, and no one is willing to do that anymore. Today kids play games on mobile devices, sitting next to each other.

It becomes critical to be mindful of the way we lead our lives and make an effort to simplify them.

A few steps I took to simplify my life

1. Replaced Kindle with physical books again.

2. Read books to avoid screen time.

3. Using a mobile phone

   a. I am back with a single smartphone with two SIMs – one official and one personal. The ringtone for both is different.

   b. Disabled all notifications.

   c. Installed only those apps that I regularly use.

   d. Keep the ringer volume low and the phone away so I don't get disturbed while working or doing something else. I can always call back.

   e. I installed Truecaller, which helps in identifying spam or unknown numbers.

   f. Implemented app timers – between 15-30 minutes maximum usage time for each app during the day. This has helped me control usage.

   g. Reducing screen brightness to help my eyes and avoid headaches and sleeplessness.

4. Set up alarms or reminders for any activity, meeting, or deliverable/task. This helps to remind me of pending things while not being in front of any device.

5. I like to work on a PC. I have set up alarms to take a break every 1 hour – get a glass of water or take a short walk.

6. What we need in life are simple things like food, water, shelter, and some medical care.

I like a simple life – simple foods, a simple lifestyle, simple clothes, simple devices, simple people, a simple car, simple house; most of my needs are simple and limited.

We often hear people say things like, "We're bored", "We want to try something new", "We want to step outside of our comfort zone", "We want to take greater risks", "No risk, no gain" etc. This is one way of looking at life. However, many of us also enjoy living in our comfort zone with safety and security. These are contrasting approaches. Pick a route that works for you.

I a\lso observe parents complicating the lives of their children by enrolling them in institutions that only emphasize academics. When 7th graders tell me that they are preparing for competitive examinations they would normally take after 12th grade, I am quite shocked. The world seems to be a competition.

Goals

My life has largely been with no major goals. I am not tuned to set goals and live by them. Most of us live this kind of life. Till I was in school, I did not know what goals meant. We were not exposed to that. Later in life, I had only three major goals in life – study MBA, buy a car, and buy a home.

Since an MBA was in demand at my time, I decided to pursue it. I finally managed to complete my MBA at a business school.

I wanted to buy a car because we never owned one in the family. It was a dream to own a car. So, I bought one seven years after I started working.

My dad worked for the government. We relocated every three years. He didn't buy a house until after he retired, and he did it in an all-cash, no-loan transaction. So, it was always in my mind to buy a home early in life and not wait till retirement. I purchased a home after marriage with a 90% loan.

Later in life, my life coach Satish Rao re-introduced me to set goals, both short and long-term.

I set monthly and yearly goals. I would tick them off as and when they were achieved, after which I would set new goals. This looked like an endless cycle of goal setting and activities to meet the new goals. Initially, it felt great to set goals and achieve them, but after a point, the process got boring. I did not enjoy doing it anymore. At times, I was setting goals for the sake of it.

After some time, I quit setting goals. This helped simplify things. If I wanted to do something, I would set a short-term goal, but for the most part, I preferred to go with the flow.

I am not saying that goal setting is not a good practice, just that it did not work for me, or I just got bored with that process. I wanted to keep myself free from any commitment, to keep it simple and flexible. Find your approach and follow it.

"Goals are ways the mind tries to control you. I need X to be happy. When I feel like I need something outside of me to be happy, I have to make room in my bag for it."

– James Altucher

Purpose or meaning of life

For a long time, I struggled to find a purpose or meaning in life. I was spiritually inclined from a young age, and I used to question everything. I do that even now.

Purpose is a motivating factor - the reason to get up every morning and work towards that purpose. Purpose can help shape life or life decisions and give a sense of direction or meaning to life. The purpose will be unique for everyone.

I still don't know if everyone is born with a purpose. Some find purpose due to life situations; some find it by accident, and for some, their purpose finds them.

I have not been able to find the true purpose of my life. If I reflect on my life – from my childhood to now, I have been going with the flow. There is nothing I could find which makes me feel that I was truly born for that.

I struggled for a long to find that purpose, but eventually gave up and realized that I needed to keep it simple and just go with the flow.

I had complicated my life on many occasions – some complications were thrown at me and were out of my control, but many were my own creations. Now I try to be more mindful and make every effort to uncomplicate or simplify.

Don't stress if you don't have a purpose or cannot find one. Just go with the flow, simplify things and lead a happy life.

There is a thin line between Goal and Purpose.

Saying NO

Saying no to tasks, activities, money, wealth, work, people, and things you don't like or have enough of it.

I have my life journey. I don't want to mess it up, trying to compete with someone else and making a hell out of my own life. My needs should determine my life, and my path should be defined accordingly. I don't want to be in a game where to win, I have to leave someone behind, or to climb, I have to pull someone down.

I don't have the urge to chase something only to discover that it isn't what I was after. I don't want to be part of that race. I want to make my own path, at my pace, at my will, and with freedom. I want to go with the flow. I believe I have my own destiny, and it is different for everyone. I want to follow the course that life has decided for me.

I prefer exploring new things, helping people, and solving problems. I would like to have the freedom of time to work on things I like, projects that I want to work on and work with people I like.

I think life is about balance—work, relationships, self-care, fun, service to others, and spirituality. Many times, we have to say no to achieve this balance.

"Saying no saves you time in the future, saying yes costs you time in the future. No is like a time credit, you can spend that block of time in the future. Yes is like a time debt, you have to repay that commitment at some point. No is a decision, yes is a responsibility."

— James Clear

Luck

Luck means success or failure, apparently brought by chance rather than through one's own actions. Luck can be good or bad, by accident or chance, for an individual or group of people. Luck plays a significant role in everyone's life.

For many years I struggled to find the reasons why few things were happening to me – good or bad. I never found the reason, and nor could I control it. The only thing which mattered was how I reacted to or dealt with that situation.

If we think logically, everyone has the same life, the same body parts, and the same amount of time, but we all live so differently – Why? Some people get lucky, and some are not so lucky. It is important to understand this and be grateful for what we have.

Lessons I learned from the gym

My trainer at the gym noted that I was moving too quickly while exercising. "Neeraj, you cannot get the desired results if you exercise so fast; you have to do it slowly and consistently," he came to me and stated one day.

It must be slow and steady. That is the key to success. We do the exact opposite. We do everything fast; we want faster results and faster gratification.

Example 1: We see people with fantastic physiques. We are unaware of the passion and effort required to create such a body. All we see is the outcome, and we want to achieve the same in a short time frame. I made that mistake too, and failed miserably.

Additional effort is required to maintain that body the way it is. To sustain the body at an optimum level takes a lot of effort.

Example 2: Look at all the successful entrepreneurs and investors. They achieved success only after putting in a lot of time and effort. We only hear about their success stories, but no one ever discusses the struggles, failures, stress, hard work, and time that went into that success.

So, keep it slow, steady, and simple.

Happiness from small things

I've always enjoyed the joy that comes from little things, whether it's eating, catching up with friends, playing with kids, having casual conversations, going out, helping others, reading, watching comedies, simply looking at the beaches, the mountains, the trees, or playing with pets.

Money does not determine our level of happiness, whether we live in a city or a village. If you go to any village, you will find people having more fun, get-togethers, celebrations, or festivals. We see people spending more time with each other as they have fewer distractions.

Small things can give big joys.

"Small is Big" says my author friend Amit Agarwal in his book of the same name.

Dealing with worry/stress

I am also learning to deal with worries and stress to simplify life. This is easier said than done.

I am a highly sensitive person by nature. I get stressed easily, ponder, and worry a lot. Not that I need to, or the situation demands it, but that is how I am wired, and it is important for me to manage it.

I try to follow the below process whenever I feel stressed:

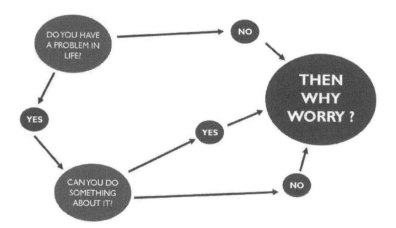

Here is how I am trying to simplify:

a. Being mindful of what I am contemplating.

b. Setting it aside if the activity/issue is not important or urgent.

c. Trying to solve the issue or manage it. Make a couple of attempts to solve it, if not, leave the problem as is and live with it until I find some solution.

d. Engaging myself in interesting things like reading, watching movies, etc, to divert my mind.

e. Avoid negative self-talk and critical questioning, especially questions like - Why doesn't someone like me? Why is someone saying bad things about me? Why did someone do this to me? Why is something bad happening only to me?

f. Reassuring myself that the world does not rest on my shoulders.

   "You can only be responsible for your own path. Let others find theirs." - Unknown

g. Not trying to correct someone even when they are wrong; making everyone perfect is not my responsibility.

h. Staying away from (office) politics and gossip. This consumes a lot of mind space. I would rather stay behind the scenes and do my work effectively.

i. Appreciate the presence of the things around me – people, animals, things, thanking the universe for their presence in my life and for making a difference. I should enjoy their presence now instead of regretting it in the future.

j. Living life for today before it becomes my last. Accepting the fact that we are not immortals, sooner or later, we all die.

k. Doing things that make me happy and not doing things that make me unhappy, realizing that I owe this to myself.

l. Not being obsessed with terminology such as success, winner, abundance, limitless, accumulate, more, compete, superior, ambition, better, special, growth

"If human beings are released from the disease of wanting to be better than someone else, life will come to ease." – Sadhguru

m. Be happy just being normal, usual, and not extraordinary.

n. Pause, slow down, disconnect (from the internet, people, information, consumption), and create solitude and space.

o. Not thinking of the past or the future. We have this life, a short one, and we have the choice to live it gracefully and with love.

p. Not comparing with others is such a great service to self. Whenever we think that we are not rich or need more, we are basically comparing ourselves with someone who has more, and such comparison is never ending and unhealthy.

"One of the most joy-robbing things you can ever do is compare your income, savings, or net worth with another person. Remember, you have a 1/7,350,000,000 chance of being the wealthiest person on the planet. If you are not the wealthiest human alive, comparing your money is always going to be a losing proposition—there is always going to be somebody with more. So don't see money as a

competition with others, see it as a competition with yourself to make the most of the little bit that you have." – Joshua Becker

q. Information diet - with information being available at our fingertips, and all apps pushing data to seek our attention, we have become addicted to information. We consume it irrespective of whether we like it or not. We are mindlessly browsing and scrolling through the information thrown at us. The monkey mind keeps jumping from one source to another. This consumes a lot of mental energy.

r. Getting rid of the idea that I need to be always busy. "If I am not doing something, then I am wasting my time." We need to get out of this mind frame.

s. Let go of the habit of controlling – controlling situations or controlling people.

t. Keep relationships with self and others simple.

u. Embrace uncertainty and insecurity.

v. Lend a helping hand with household chores.

w. Avoid multitasking and do things slowly.

It's okay not to be perfect

When I was younger, I believed that when I grew up, life would be wonderful. When I grew up, I thought life would be better when I start earning. When I started earning, I thought life would be even better if I earn more. Then, when I started making more money, I felt life would be good if I could save enough to support myself and my family when I retired.

We are always looking forward to that future perfect day. Despite working for so many years, I have yet to achieve this stage. Do you know why? – Because it was never enough! I always thought the future was better and ignored the present. In many cases, I felt the past was better. Do you feel the same? Well, many of us feel this way.

While you make plans, live for the moment as well. Don't disregard what you already have. We've learned our lessons from the pandemic. There is no assurance of life for anyone. So, instead of focusing solely on the future, relish the here and now.

If I were to die today, is there something I would regret, or is there unfinished business? These are my current reflections. I want to live a normal life without much pressure with absolute peace and calmness and cherish every moment.

My goal is to live an intentional and meaningful life. So, let's stop running, pause and review the kind of life we want.

Complexity of Choices

Humans are spoilt with choices, but that doesn't necessarily make life more comfortable. On the contrary, it might have made our lives more complicated.

I would like to touch upon various aspects of life that might have made my life complicated if I had not made some conscious decisions.

"Autonomy and freedom of choice are critical to our well-being, and choice is critical to freedom and autonomy. Nonetheless, though modern Americans have more choice than any group of people ever has before, and thus, presumably, more freedom and autonomy, we don't seem to be benefiting from it psychologically". Barry Schwartz

The Paradox of Choice – Why More Is Less is a book written by American psychologist Barry Schwartz. In the book, Schwartz argues that eliminating consumer choices can greatly reduce anxiety for shoppers. The book analyses the behavior of different types of people (in particular, maximizers and satisficers) facing the rich choice.

"Maximizers are people who want the very best. *Satisficers* are people who want good enough," says Barry Schwartz.

This book demonstrates how the dramatic explosion in choice - from the mundane things to the profound challenges of balancing career, family, and individual needs - has paradoxically become a problem instead of a solution and how our obsession with choice encourages us to seek that which makes us feel worse.

How I simplified life by restricting choices:

1. *Clothes*: Clothing is amongst our biggest living expenses. We are obsessed with dressing up stylishly with designer clothing. Our obsession with brands defines who we are. People judge us based on the brands we wear or carry.

   Celebrities get trolled for wearing the same clothes on two occasions or two celebrities wearing the same design. Imagine how stressful and complicated their life must be.

   We buy clothes for every occasion. Formals, semi-formals, festivals, weddings, parties, sports, vacations, business, casual, social media, and even for the airport look. There is a dress for everything.

   To keep life simple, I wear the same color and brand of clothing every day. I don't have to spend time on what I need to wear or what I have to buy, because I have simplified my shopping process.

2. *Food*: The time we discussed regional cuisine or specialties has long passed. These days, we discuss international cuisines. Again, the options are endless. There are countless variations. When you visit a food court or a restaurant serving a variety of cuisines, you will get a sense of it. Choosing food can be really challenging.

   This is how I simplified my food choices:

   a. Eat 3-4 dishes on rotation for breakfast and lunch.

   b. Porridge or something very light every evening.

c. Seasonal fruits in between.

Even when we have to order a meal for home delivery or go to a restaurant, we already know exactly where we want to go (out of the few restaurants we have shortlisted) and what we want to eat. We also know exactly what we don't want to eat.

We have been purchasing food from the same stores for many years and the same brands. As a result, we always know where to buy and what to buy.

3. *Cosmetics*: There are countless options available in this area as well. However, not for me. I don't use any cosmetics, luxury soaps, shampoos, conditioners, after-shave, shaving cream, or other products. The only cosmetic I use is perfume and toothpowder, and I have been using the same brand for many years. That's it. It is that simple.

4. *Finance*: I have explained this in detail in the first chapter. One bank account, one credit card with restricted use and credit limit, one medical insurance, two term insurance policies, expertly managed investments, and tax filing managed by professionals. This has been my attempt to simplify.

5. *Motor vehicle*: There are many manufacturers, showrooms, brands, and choices. People in my immediate circle have been known to spend days and even weeks looking into the vehicles available, reading reviews, taking test drives, haggling, making decisions, and then having to confront a long waiting period. Life gets complicated with so many choices. A lot of time and effort goes into just the selection process.

I know people who change their cars every 2-3 years, and each time they spend the same amount of time and effort choosing a new one.

I used my first car for 10 years. The second car, the one I am currently using, is 7 years old. When purchasing my second vehicle, I ensured I got it from the same manufacturer and had a clear idea of the model and color I wanted. Just to be sure, I went for a test drive once. So, it just took me a day to decide.

I have been using the same two-wheeler for the last 16 years.

I do sometimes get thoughts of upgrading my car or two-wheeler, but then I postpone that thought and get pragmatic. Simple is ample.

6. *Trading*: As mentioned in the previous chapters, I had complicated my trading business by using way too many indicators and methods of trading.

So, many tools, strategies, and trading styles - day trading, swing trading, momentum, positional, futures and options, so many stocks, so many platforms, and so many experts with their own styles and opinions. A normal human being will only get confused and run through this paradox of choices.

It took me a couple of years to realize how I had complicated my trading business and did a course correction. Now I have considerably simplified trading.

7. *Relationships*: Every relationship needs time and effort to flourish. Every relationship is unique and needs equal attention.

There is one relationship that we don't get to choose, and that is the parent-child relationship and the relatives who come by default with this relationship. But you have a choice in every other relationship – be it friends, spouse, or employer-employee.

Be it a personal or professional relationship, one must put in the effort to make it work. Some relationships work, and others don't. We have a choice to stay or not to stay in a relationship. If it gets toxic, adversely affecting both sides even after making efforts to correct it, then it is better to cut that relationship and lead a better life.

I, too, made my choices in relationships and simplified them.

8. *Work*: I keep my work life simple. In the 25 years of my career, I have spent 22 years with just two companies. I did not look for choices. I am quite happy with my work and the people I work with.

In this respect, we can learn from the experiences of our fathers and grandfathers. They spent the whole of their working careers in the same company or organization. Yes, there were fewer opportunities, but life back then was easy and simple.

People who have for many years been employed in the same business/organization are becoming uncommon. Like changing their automobiles, people switch jobs every couple of years, and it's considered cool. A career shift is regarded as a step forward in life.

So, make your choices carefully and keep your work life simple.

9. *Home*: Of course, we should take our time to choose or build the ideal home for us to live in. But with the options we now have, making decisions has grown extremely challenging.

Decision-making was easier in the past. You purchased a piece of land and constructed a house to live there. However, no one has the time now to acquire the land and construct a house.

We have plenty of construction companies, multiple projects, and many options now.

The decision-making process to buy a house has become complicated with so many choices and variables to consider.

To simplify, we decided to stay in a rented house for at least the next few years.

"Sometimes you need to move slowly, so you can then move powerfully. The modern world is so fast paced that you feel the pressure to keep up. Setting aside what everyone else is doing and moving at your natural speed will help you make better decisions and lift up your inner peace."

— Yung Pueblo

Hedonic Treadmill Theory

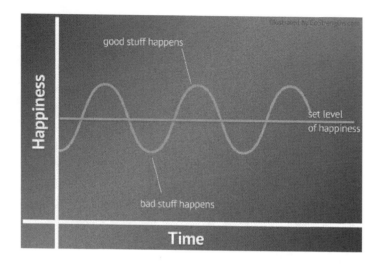

There are both good and bad times in life. We experience a range of emotions and feelings. However, none of these endure. We continually return to the constant (or the baseline, the mean) level of emotion or enjoyment.

It is very important to comprehend this. We eventually return to a neutral level of happiness no matter how much money we earn, how much we consume, or how big a house or automobile we have.

So why do we worry or struggle so much if we must eventually return to base? Why can't we just make everything simpler?

I had seen this somewhere, and I liked what is visualised.

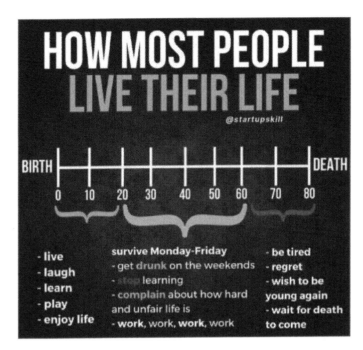

It is entirely our choice – to make what we want out of this life and how we want to live it.

Eventually, everyone's life goal is to have a peaceful and happy life.

Life is amazingly good when its simple and amazingly simple when its good.

– Terri Guillemets

Conclusion

You probably are thinking now that everything is simplified in my life, the life I lead must be sorted and perfect. Well, the answer is both yes and no.

There is no such thing as a perfect life. It is a journey mixed with different experiences.

Yes, a significant portion of my life has been organized, streamlined, and simplified. I experienced numerous ups and downs on my voyage as well. I understood what was ample for me and that helped in making things better and simple.

No, since we need to cope with new challenges every day. There are new experiences every day, and we must go through them and adapt to new situations.

All great and successful people said the same thing over and over again - Take care of your health, be kind to others, and spend more time with family; nothing else is more important. Are we listening?

I desired to uncomplicate and simplify my life. Simple things have always brought me joy, be it simple cuisine, simple clothing, a simple home, a simple car, simple people, or simple things.

Simple is ample for me, what is it for you?

Share your story and how you have simplified your life. Would love to hear from you and learn. Write to me on neeraj.deginal@ gmail.com

Our life is frittered away by detail. Simplify, simplify.

– Henry David Thoreau

Disclaimer

*A*ll investment decisions mentioned in the book were made based on my needs and personal research. I am not connected to any investment firm or individual. Please do your own research before investing.

Also, it is not necessary, what worked for me, would work for you as well. Based on your personal situation and requirement, you can try different methods to simplify.

Acknowledgment

$\mathcal{T}$hanking with gratitude

Parents, family, in-laws, Dr. Deepak, Achal Khanna, all my wonderful colleagues, Samrat, Robin Ramakrishna, friends & relatives, Siddhi Jain, and the Cleverfox team.

Manufactured by Amazon.ca
Bolton, ON

33018124R00067